THIS WALKER BOOK BELONGS TO:

Natasha Mariyah

For "T"

First published 2002 by Walker Books Ltd
87 Vauxhall Walk, London SE11 5HJ

This edition published 2003

4 6 8 10 9 7 5 3

© 2002 Sue Heap

The right of Sue Heap to be identified as author/illustrator
of this work has been asserted by her in accordance with
the Copyright, Designs and Patents Act 1988

This book has been typeset in 'ela' Tapioca Semi-Bold

Printed in China

British Library Cataloguing in Publication Data:
a catalogue record for this book
is available from the British Library

ISBN 978-0-7445-9497-3

www.walker.co.uk

Let's Play Fairies!

Sue Heap

WALKER BOOKS
AND SUBSIDIARIES
LONDON · BOSTON · SYDNEY · AUCKLAND

"Let's play fairies," said Lily May.

"No, let's play trees," said Matt.

Martha
was a
shaky
tree.

Matt
was a
big tree.

Lily May
was a
quiet
tree.

Then all three of them were a row of trees reaching for the sky.

"Now let's play fairies," said Lily May.

"No," said Matt, "because we're going to play..."

Matt
was a
bumpy
car.

Lily May
was a
steady car.

Martha
was a
fast car.

Then all three of them were poop-poop cars in a traffic jam.

"Now let's play fairies," said Lily May.

Martha was a slow cat.

Matt was a sleepy cat.

Lily May was a creeping cat.

Then all three of them were noisy, meowing and washing-their-whiskers cats.

"Now we're going to be wibbly-wobbly jellies," said Matt.

And they were.

"Now let's play fairies," said Lily May. "I've got a magic wand!"

All three of them
were fairies and
they could fly.

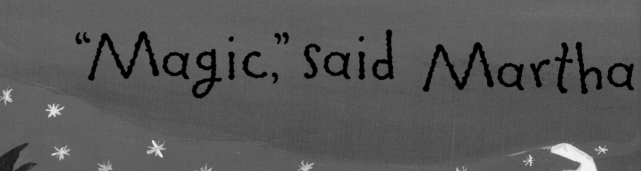

"Magic," said Martha

"That was fun," said Matt.

"I love playing fairies!"
said Lily May.

WALKER BOOKS is the world's leading independent
publisher of children's books. Working with
the best authors and illustrators we create books
for all ages, from babies to teenagers – books your child
will grow up with and always remember. So…

FOR THE BEST CHILDREN'S BOOKS, LOOK FOR THE BEAR